THE PERFECTIONIST

THE BEDMAKER

SLEAZY JIM

MR LATE

BUSINESSMAN

THE FORCED

THE BROKEN-HEARTED MAN

THE CLOCK

THE FACE

THE S
BU

D0294813

Andrew Kaufman

ALL MY FRIENDS ARE
SUPERHEROES

TELEGRAM

Published 2013 by Telegram

First published in Great Britain in 2006 by Telegram

TELEGRAM
26 Westbourne Grove, London W2 5RH
www.telegrambooks.com

First published in Canada in 2003 by Coach House Books

A full CIP record for this book is available
from the British Library.

ISBN 978-1-84659-160-0
eISBN 978-1-84659-163-1

Printed and bound by Bookwell, Finland

Cover design and illustrations by James Nunn

for Marlo

ONE

DESIGNATED WAITING AREA

Tom and the Perfectionist sit in the designated waiting area of Gate 23, Terminal 2, Lester B. Pearson International Airport. It's 10:13 a.m. Tom watches the Perfectionist check the address on her carry-on luggage. She tugs the tag. It's the third time she's done this. She looks around the airport lounge. There are more people than seats. She can't figure out why no one has taken the empty chair to her right.

The chair to her right isn't empty. Tom sits in this chair. To the Perfectionist, Tom is invisible. He's been trying to convince her he isn't since August 14th, their wedding night, six months ago. Tom has whispered and

7

shouted. He's made phone calls and sent faxes, telegrams and e-mails. Mutual friends have tried to convince her that Tom isn't invisible. They can see him. She can't. Tom is invisible only to the Perfectionist.

They have fifteen minutes before boarding flight AC117 to Vancouver. The Perfectionist is completely unaware that Tom's beside her. He touches the back of her head; the Perfectionist begins to hiccup. Whenever Tom touches her head, she hiccups. When he touches her leg she has muscle spasms. Touching her back makes her sneeze. Tom takes his hand away from her head and puts it in his lap. The Perfectionist stops hiccuping.

Their relationship has never been simple. The Perfectionist is a superhero. The source of her power is her need for order. She needs it so badly she can will it to happen with her mind. Tom isn't a superhero, although the Perfectionist isn't the first superhero he's dated.

Tom's first superhero girlfriend was Someday. She had red hair, a compact frame and two superpowers: an amazing ability to think big and an unlimited capacity to procrastinate. Someday had never used her superpowers in combination until one Sunday morning, three months after she'd started dating Tom. They were lying in bed. Someday was staring at the ceiling.

'Imagine it all,' Someday said.

'Hmmm,' Tom said. He kissed Someday's freckled shoulder.

'We're going to get married and own a home. We're going to have kids …' she said.

Tom stopped kissing her freckled shoulder. He stopped moving his fingers. They could hear the refrigerator.

'… someday,' Someday quickly added.

The moment she said it, she shrank. It started happening all the time.

'I'm going to paint the bathroom …' she'd say.

'Don't say it!' Tom would yell.

'… someday,' Someday would say. She'd shrink.

Every time Someday used her superpowers in combination she shrank, and every time she shrank, she shrank by a little bit more. When they'd met in March, Someday stood 5' 4". By May she was 4' 7". At the end of August she was 11". By October she was sleeping on the cotton from a bottle of aspirin.

The last time Tom saw her was in December, through a microscope. She stood next to a dust particle.

'Someday, I miss you!' Tom told her.

'Someday you won't,' she said.

She disappeared.

Tom's second superhero girlfriend was TV Girl. As a child, TV Girl loved television. She could empathize with the people on television in ways she couldn't with real-life people. She watched so much television, caring so much about the people she watched, that her connection with television became biological. She started crying televisions. When TV Girl was sad, little television sets would flow down her face.

Tom wasn't very nice to TV Girl. He didn't have a television. He'd go over to her apartment and be mean to her just to watch her cry.

At his own wedding reception, Tom was introduced to the Sitcom Kid. Tom didn't know the Sitcom Kid was TV Girl's older brother. Tom stuck out his hand to be shaken. The Sitcom Kid made a fist and punched Tom in the mouth.

'She's my sister, man!' said the Sitcom Kid.

'Who is?' Tom asked.

'TV Girl! You made her feel like Mallory when she dated Alex's best friend at university.'

Tom held a paper napkin to his lip. He didn't swing back. He knew he deserved that punch in the mouth – maybe not on his wedding night, but he deserved that punch. All the wedding guests circled Tom and the Sitcom Kid. Hypno knew this was his moment.

Only the Perfectionist noticed Hypno making his way towards her. She wasn't afraid of him. She knew how he worked. He'd done it the first time they'd met. He'd come into the diner where she worked. He'd sat by himself at the counter, just as the noon crowd had her swamped.

'I need coffee,' Hypno commanded. He waved his hand in front of her face. He hypnotized her.

The Perfectionist dropped everything. Plates of

hamburgers got cold under heat lamps as she made a new pot just for him. She filled a mug and took it directly to Hypno. She set it down in front of him.

'How did you do that?' the Perfectionist asked.

'You're a nice person,' Hypno answered.

'So?'

'You wanted to give me good service.'

'So?'

'I hypnotized you. But you can't hypnotize anyone into doing anything they don't already want to do. I merely give permission,' Hypno said. He tapped his spoon on the rim of his coffee mug and hypnotized her into believing that sex with him would be the best of her life. The Perfectionist dated him, intensely, for the next three months.

'Just because you were hypnotized to think it was the best sex of your life doesn't mean that it wasn't,' is how the Perfectionist remembers their relationship. For Hypno, the feelings went much, much deeper. He was still in love with the Perfectionist when he approached her at the wedding reception.

The Perfectionist stood still. His timing was perfect; a brawl had broken out by the shrimp table. If he made some sort of scene, nobody would notice. Hypno hugged her. She hugged him back. It was her wedding day. She didn't need anybody's permission to do anything.

'Congratulations,' he whispered.

'What?' asked the Perfectionist.

'Congratulations,' he whispered, even more softly.

'What?' the Perfectionist asked again. She couldn't hear him. She turned her head. She offered her ear to Hypno. He leaned close and whispered.

Only the Ear heard what Hypno said. The Ear was in the bathroom changing the cotton in his ears. He'd just pulled out the used cotton. He had fresh cotton in his hand. His hearing was at its most sensitive.

The Ear heard the fight between Tom and the Sitcom Kid. He heard someone whispering behind it.

'Are you worried that he's not like us?' the Ear heard. He recognized Hypno's voice. The Ear didn't know who Hypno was talking to. The other person wasn't saying anything.

The Perfectionist wasn't saying anything because she was thinking. She had never been asked that question before and she realized she'd never let herself even think about it. She bit her bottom lip. She nodded her head.

'What do you see in him?' Hypno asked.

'I … I … don't know,' the Perfectionist replied. She knew she loved Tom but she suddenly didn't know why.

Hearing the Perfectionist's voice, the Ear rushed out of the bathroom. He tried to push through the crowd encircling Tom and the Sitcom Kid. He kept listening.

'In fact,' the Ear heard Hypno whisper, 'I don't think you see anything at all.'

'Perf, no!' called the Ear.

But the Ear was too late. The Perfectionist was hypnotized. Tom was invisible to her.

TWO

ALL HIS FRIENDS ARE SUPERHEROES

A group of children, all holding hands and wearing identical blue T-shirts, walk past Tom. He leans forward in the uncomfortable airport chair and watches them walk away. Careful not to touch her, Tom bends close to the Perfectionist. 'Please see me,' he pleads. 'You have to see me by the time we land in Vancouver.'

This is true. The Perfectionist is moving to Vancouver. She's shipped her belongings and rented an apartment. As soon as flight AC117 touches down in Vancouver, she'll leave everything, Tom included, behind. All the pain, all the heartache, all the love she has for him, will disappear. She'll make Vancouver perfect. She has the power to do this. It's been six months since he disappeared. Six months is long enough.

It was the Amphibian who pulled Tom off Hypno that night. He let Tom get in five punches. Hypno was down and his nose was bloody. The Amphibian decided five was enough. He grabbed Tom's arms and pulled him off Hypno.

Tom resisted. The Amphibian had to use all his strength to keep Tom's arms pinned behind his back.

'One more!' Tom called.

'It's not going to help,' the Amphibian said.

'One more!' Tom said.

'It will not help,' the Amphibian said.

Tom's arms went limp. He stopped resisting. Hypno smirked. Tom spat in Hypno's face. He hadn't wanted to invite Hypno to the wedding in the first place.

The Amphibian and Tom are best friends now, but when Tom moved into town, he didn't know anybody. He'd taken a job as a pool cleaner. The season was ending and Tom had nothing else lined up. He was draining a pool he hadn't cleaned as scheduled. The water had a murky green hue. The people who owned the pool had been away for months and they were coming back the next day. The pool had to be dry and something was clogging the drain at the bottom.

Tom took off his shoes. He took off his shorts and shirt. He dove naked into the pool and swam to the bottom.

The chemicals made it impossible to keep his eyes open. He felt around with his hands. His fingers found something slimy. It was firm in the middle but the top layer felt soft. Tom pulled. Whatever it was was really stuck.

Tom put his feet on the bottom of the pool, got his legs into it and freed whatever it was. He squinted his eyes open. What he saw made him gasp. He swallowed a mouthful of chlorine pool water, then raced for the surface as fast as he could.

It easily beat him. It slipped out of the pool.

Tom didn't want to get out of the pool knowing it was waiting for him. He swam around, trying to figure out what to do. Eventually he ran out of breath and had to break the surface.

'Thanks!' the Amphibian said.

Tom looked at the Amphibian's green skin, webbed feet and webbed hands. He'd thought it was about to rip him limb from limb, and relief flooded through him when this didn't happen.

'No problem,' Tom answered.

'What's your superpower?' the Amphibian asked.

'Superpower?'

'Yeah, you know. Your superpower.'

'I don't have one,' Tom told him. 'I'm just regular.'

'Really?' the Amphibian said.

Tom swam over to the side of the pool. They shook hands.

The Amphibian introduced Tom to all his friends. All the Amphibian's friends were superheroes. The Amphibian's friends became Tom's friends. Now all of Tom's friends are superheroes. But because they all have a superpower, and everyone they know has a superpower, having a superpower is nothing special to them. What's special to them is not having a superpower. They can't imagine how anyone could get through life without having a superpower. It seems unbelievable to them.

'Now boarding rows 14 through 34. Rows 14 through 34 now boarding,' the airline representative announces.

The Perfectionist picks up her carry-on luggage. She stands in line. Tom waits in his seat. He hates standing in any line he doesn't have to; the Perfectionist can't watch any line she could be standing in. At this stage, they would have been separated anyway.

THREE

AMBROSE HEART-REPAIR SERVICE

For the first week of invisibility Tom did nothing but follow her around. There are perks to having your lover believe you're invisible. He watched the Perfectionist dress and undress. He watched what she watched on television when she thought he wasn't around – mainly game shows and reruns. He watched her separate the coloured laundry into shades. In ways, his invisibility let him be more intimate with her but safer at the same time, and he fell deeper in love with her.

Four weeks after the reception, a Wednesday, the Perfectionist came home with a packet of cigarettes. She had never smoked before. She took to it quickly.

She began smoking at the kitchen table, smoke rings floating through the kitchen. For four straight days the Perfectionist sat at the kitchen table blowing smoke rings across the room. Her fingers turned yellow. She did nothing else. She waited for Tom.

That night Tom started having pains in his chest. The first one came at ten in the evening. It was sharp and enduring. He doubled over but it passed. The next came two hours later; by morning they came every ten minutes. The Perfectionist was sleeping and he knew not to touch her. He called the Amphibian.

'Hey,' said Tom.

'Hey,' said the Amphibian.

'Ahhhh,' said Tom. A pain shot through his heart.

'What's happening?'

'Pain in my chest.'

'Sharp and enduring?'

'Yes.'

'But recurring?'

'Yes!'

'In greater frequency?'

'Less than ten minutes now.'

'I'm sending over a doctor.'

'What is it?'

'He's the best there is.'

'Tell me what it is!'

'Your heart is breaking,' the Amphibian said.

It took Ambrose, the Amphibian's doctor, ten minutes to arrive at Tom's door.

Ambrose's hands were thick. His fingers were muscular and the knuckles bulbous, well oiled. He pulled a red rag from his back pocket and mopped his face. 'You the guy with the heart?' he asked Tom.

'Yes.'

Ambrose took off his baseball cap. He put it back on his head. He raised his eyebrows. 'I ain't got all day ...'

Tom backed out of the doorway.

'Where's the kitchen?' Ambrose asked.

Tom led Ambrose through the living room into the kitchen. Ambrose's eyes went to the kitchen table.

'This sturdy?' Ambrose inquired, leaning all his weight on the corner of the table. He kneeled and inspected the joints underneath. 'It'll have to do,' he said and started clearing the breakfast dishes and newspapers. 'Strip,' he commanded.

Tom started unbuttoning.

Ambrose pointed to the kitchen table. 'Face down,' he said.

Tom climbed onto the kitchen table. He was naked. The linoleum tabletop was cold on his cheek.

Ambrose snapped a rubber glove over his right hand. He put one finger up Tom's anus. Tom gasped. Ambrose pulled up and Tom felt a *pop* in his chest. Ambrose turned him over and Tom saw how his chest had released, come open like the hood of a car. Ambrose raised Tom's chest, propping it open with a rib bone at a forty-five-degree angle. He started poking around in there.

'Think about your girlfriend,' Ambrose commanded.

'My wife,' Tom said.

'Whatever, just picture her face.'

Tom pictured the Perfectionist's face.

'Now picture her best feature,' Ambrose instructed.

Tom pictured the Perfectionist's nose. He felt Ambrose's hand on his heart. Tom took shallow breaths. Ambrose reached behind his heart. He squeezed from underneath and a quick line of blood squirted up, hitting Ambrose in the face.

'That might be it,' Ambrose said, reaching to his back pocket, grabbing the rag and wiping off his face.

'What? What is it?'

'When's the last time you had this cleaned?'

'I've never had it cleaned.'

'Exactly,' Ambrose said. 'I'll need the Stewart for this.'

The Stewart was a long, unwieldy tool Ambrose rarely used and kept in the back of his truck. Leaving Tom naked on the kitchen table, Ambrose left the room.

Tom listened to the apartment door open and close. Ambrose was gone for fifteen minutes. Tom lay naked on the kitchen table. He craned his neck down and to the right and watched his heart beating.

Ambrose returned carrying a long metal toolbox. He

21

took out an instrument that was long and sharp and made of thin stainless steel. This was the Stewart. Ambrose used two hands to hold it.

'Take a deep breath,' Ambrose instructed. 'And think of the first time you kissed her.'

Tom pictured the horrible basement apartment he used to live in. The worst thing was the linoleum floor in the kitchen. Boot scuffs and cigarette burns covered it. No longer white, it was a grey that always looked dirty.

The Perfectionist couldn't stand it. One Wednesday, five days after their first official date, she showed up with two buckets of bright blue floor paint and two paint rollers.

'Great idea,' Tom said.

They set to painting the floor. They started where the carpet hit the linoleum. They worked backwards at a furious pace. They'd paint what was in front of them, then shuffle back a few feet and paint that. In no time at all their feet hit the back wall of the kitchen. They'd painted themselves into a corner. Tom looked up and the Perfectionist was smiling.

'What the hell do we do now?' Tom asked her.

The Perfectionist kissed him (perfectly).

Tom remembered this moment as he felt the instrument push down his aorta. The pain was unbelievably sharp. Tom opened his eyes. He craned his neck. He saw a tiny ghost coming out of his heart.

Tom recognized the ghost as Jessica Kenmore.

Her head, then her chest, her hips and finally her legs squeezed out of his heart. She floated upwards, dissolving just before she touched the ceiling.

Ambrose pushed the instrument deeper. The head of Sally Morgan appeared. Sally's chest, then her feet came clear. She floated up, dissolving just before reaching the ceiling.

Next came Nancy Wallenstine. Then Sara Livingston. Then Debbie Cook.

'Christ, how many do you have in there?' Ambrose called.

'There should be one more,' Tom told him.

Tom gripped the edge of the kitchen table. He clenched his teeth. Ambrose pushed the instrument deeper. The head of Jenny Remington popped out of his heart.

Jenny Remington pulled herself free. She floated over to Tom's head. She stared at him. She looked so sad. She continued staring him in the eyes, then dissolved.

Tom closed his eyes. He took a deep, deep breath. He could feel the Stewart every time his heart beat.

'Well, that didn't work,' Ambrose said, pulling the Stewart out of Tom's heart.

'What?'

'Still broken. Good that you cleaned her out. You won't be getting those pains any more, but she's still broken.'

'Can't you fix it?'

'Nope. The whole thing's broken, and when she breaks

23

like that, there's nothing anyone can do,' Ambrose said, wiping the Stewart clean with the cloth from his back pocket. 'Maybe it'll mend itself. Sometimes they do.'

Ambrose set the rib bone back into place. He held the hood of Tom's chest with the tips of his fingers and let it drop. Ambrose packed up his tools. He shook his head, didn't say a word, and left.

FOUR

REGULARS

'All passengers are reminded to present proper identification with their boarding passes,' the airline representative announces through the PA system. 'Proper identification must be presented with your boarding pass.'

Tom reaches into his jacket pocket. He has proper ID and a boarding pass for flight AC117. His seat, E27, is beside the Perfectionist's. But he hasn't shipped his belongings to Vancouver. He's paid another month on their apartment. His ticket is a return ticket.

Tom is so desperate he's secretly hoping he's a superhero. He's never hoped for this before. There's a chance he might be. All superheroes are born superheroes, but some of them, for part of their lives, appear regular. Their superpowers are inside them, dormant, waiting for the right event to trigger them. Tom doesn't know how else he'll make the Perfectionist see him.

He puts his ID and boarding pass back in his jacket pocket. He thinks about the Shadowless Man.

Before the Shadowless Man was the Shadowless Man, he was Henry Zimmerman. He was regular. He always knew when the toast was going to pop. He routinely opened the telephone book to exactly the right page when looking for a phone number and was always finding money on the street. But nothing incredibly strange, nothing that'd suggest he was a superhero, had ever happened.

Then one Wednesday he woke up at 6:34 a.m. This was early for Henry Zimmerman. His shadow was sitting on the edge of his bed.

'I'm leaving you,' his shadow told him.

Zimmerman leaned on his elbow. He studied his shadow. It looked so tiny.

'Are you unhappy?' he asked his shadow.

'Yes.'

'Then you should go.'

Zimmerman's shadow hesitated. Almost imperceptibly, it nodded. It pushed itself to its feet. It walked across the room and closed the bedroom door behind itself.

Henry Zimmerman was now the Shadowless Man. That night he made his wife fettuccini alfredo. It was the first time he'd cooked for her in two and a half years. They had wine. He made her laugh. They'd opened a second bottle by the time they went to bed.

The Shadowless Man started jogging. Domestic chores like vacuuming became almost fun. On particularly sunny days, the Shadowless Man will look down and notice the absence of his shadow. He'll remember his shadow fondly and briefly wonder where it could be. But it doesn't happen that often.

Businessman was also once regular. He was Lewis Taylor until his BMW began billowing smoke during rush hour in the heart of the financial district. It was a cold Wednesday morning, − 17 °C plus wind chill. Cars were conking out all over town. The Canadian Automobile Association was backed up.

Lewis sat in his car, waiting for the tow, rubbing his arms and stamping his feet. He didn't listen to the radio. He was afraid of draining the battery. He had nothing to do but watch the pedestrians. He decided to guess how much money they were worth.

The first pedestrian who walked by was an elderly woman wearing a long wool overcoat. Lewis tried to guess her net worth and discovered he didn't need to. He could see through her clothes, into her wallet and counted seventeen dollars in cash. He discovered he could see into her bank card, into her bank account. She had four hundred dollars in savings and was overdrawn in chequing.

Lewis Taylor had become Businessman. The tow truck still hadn't arrived. Businessman sat in his car calculating the net worth of everyone who passed and he noticed something peculiar. While some people were worth millions and other people were deep in debt, they all looked stressed and worried. He concluded that there is only one amount of money – just not enough.

The only other once-regular Tom knows is the Impossible Man. The Impossible Man was Ted Wilcox until one Wednesday in April. Ted had spent the last thirteen months trying to build fires underwater. Before that he'd spent three years failing to develop methods of preserving steam. Before that he'd spent a year trying to walk on water. Ted was walking down the street when he suddenly realized that all these things were impossible. And he should stop doing them.

Tom sinks into his plastic designated-waiting-area chair. He wishes this were a Wednesday. But it isn't. It's Tuesday.

FALLING GIRL

Falling Girl won't go higher than the second floor of any building. She's never set foot on a balcony and the floor is the only place she'll sit. A small sample of things she's fallen from includes trees, cars, grace, first-storey windows, horses, ladders, bicycles, the wagon, countless kitchen counters and her grandmother's knee.

Smoking beside the Ear one winter night, she wiggled deeper under the sheets and admitted the only thing she's never fallen from, or into, was love. 'If that's how you do it, I would have done it,' she said. Then she leaned over to butt out her cigarette and fell out of the bed.

THE BATTERY

All through her youth, the Battery had two things: an overpowering father and an over-rebellious mind. In combination, these forces gave her the ability to store great amounts of emotional energy and release it in one blinding bolt. But beware: the Battery's allegiances aren't to good or evil, but simply against whatever stands in her way. Friend, foe or innocent bystander – the Battery's emotional energy bursts are unpredictable and she will strike at will.

THE COUCH SURFER

Empowered with the ability to sustain life and limb without a job, steady companion or permanent place of residence, the Couch Surfer can be found roaming from couch to couch of friends' apartments all across the city.

The Couch Surfer is not only able to withstand long

periods of acute poverty but is also able to nutritionally sustain himself with only handfuls of breakfast cereals, slices of dry bread and condiments. Mysteriously, he always has cigarettes.

THE STRESS BUNNY

If you arrive at a party and suddenly find yourself completely relaxed, there's a good chance the Stress Bunny is there. Blessed with the ability to absorb the stress of everyone in a fifty-foot radius, the Stress Bunny is invited to every party, every outing.

Her power originates from her strict Catholic upbringing.

THE DANCER

The Dancer has direct communication with God, much like a personal phone line. The telephone she uses is her body and she dials by dancing. As such, her dancing is a very, very sensual thing.

In the past, whenever she went out dancing, she got hit on and hit on and hit on. She didn't like this at all. She hated it. It wasn't what she was trying to do. She just wanted to talk to God. She almost gave up dancing altogether. Then she got an idea.

Now, just before she goes out dancing, the Dancer straddles a photocopier and makes copies of her vagina. When guys come up and hit on her, she just hands them a copy.

FIVE

THE ANXIETY MONSTER

The Perfectionist still hasn't boarded. Tom watches her wait in line. She takes a baby step. She sets down her luggage. She waits for the man in front of her to take a baby step. He does. The Perfectionist picks up her carry-on, swings it over her shoulder and takes a baby step. She sets down her carry-on. She waits.

Tom squirms in the plastic chair and looks away. He could never do what she's doing. It would fill him with anxiety, something Tom learned to avoid at the end of his first official date with the Perfectionist.

The dinner had been Italian. The movie had been black

32

and white. On the walk home, their arms brushed three times. She invited him up and made coffee. They sat four inches apart on the Perfectionist's white sofa.

The Perfectionist tilted her head slightly to the right. Tom swallowed. She leaned towards him. She closed her eyes. Someone knocked on her door.

'Just ignore it and it'll go away,' the Perfectionist said. She leaned in closer. Tom felt her breath on his lips. There was another knock.

'I'll … I'll get it,' Tom said.

The Perfectionist sighed. Tom wiped his hands on his jeans. He got off the couch and opened the door. He had almost no time to react – the monster at the door was struggling to claw his face off.

Tom slammed the door shut. He locked it. He put his back to it. The thing started screaming. It sounded like a blender.

'Was it tall?' the Perfectionist asked him.

'What?' Tom yelled. The thing was screaming very loudly.

'Was it tall?'

'Yes!'

'Pointed fingernails?'

'Yes!'

'Long, scabby arms?'

'Yes!'

'It smelled like cigarettes and cough syrup?'

'That's it!'

'That's an anxiety monster,' she said. 'I'm having a bath.'

'What?' Tom screamed.

'It's for you, not me. I'm having a bath,' she stated. Tom didn't reply. His back remained firmly pressed to her front door. She saw the look of terror in his eyes.

'Do you love me?' she asked him.

Tom did love her. He'd been in love with her for four months. He could remember the day it had happened. It had snowed overnight and the linoleum floor was cold under his feet. Tom wore nothing but a terry-cloth housecoat. As he got to the door, she knocked again (perfectly). He knew it was the Perfectionist. Did he have time to shower? Brush his teeth? At the very least try to comb down his bed-head?

'Tom?' the Perfectionist asked through the door. Her voice was sad and worried and small. Tom opened the door. The Perfectionist looked up. Snow melted and fell off her boots onto the hallway carpet. She raised her hand and waved it over Tom's head. Instantly, his hair was perfect. It was the best hair he'd ever had. He invited her in.

The Perfectionist sat down on the edge of the armchair. She started biting her thumbnail. She didn't know why she was there. 'Why Tom's?' she asked herself. She didn't know him that well. Why hadn't she gone to the Amphibian's or to Hypno, her boyfriend?

'What's wrong?' Tom asked.

'It's the snow,' she said. 'I can't organize the snowflakes.'

Tom wasn't in love with her yet; he just had a crush on her, so he wondered why she'd want to do such a thing. But he got dressed and they went outside to look at the snow. Four inches had fallen. Everything was covered. The sidewalks weren't cleared and people were walking through the snow, leaving trails behind them.

'I tried to organize them but I couldn't,' she said. Her eyes were full moons. She seemed to have stopped blinking. Tom didn't know what to do.

'Just close your eyes,' Tom told the Perfectionist.

'But I still see them,' the Perfectionist told Tom. She started shaking uncontrollably.

'Why don't we try this,' Tom said.

He motioned to his car. He helped the Perfectionist into the passenger seat. He started the engine, turned on the heater and brushed off the snow. Tom drove out of the city, into the country, and stopped his car in front of a field completely covered in undisturbed snow. No animals or people – nothing but the wind – had been across it. Tom helped the Perfectionist out of the car. They stood looking at the field of snow.

'Can you organize these snowflakes?' he asked her.

'They already are,' she said. It was at that exact moment that Tom fell in love with her.

Tom remembered standing there beside her, in front of that field covered with snow, and falling in love. The Anxiety Monster screamed again.

'Do you love me?' the Perfectionist repeated.

'Yes,' Tom said.

'Then trust me. I'm going to have a bath.'

The Perfectionist got off the couch. She walked around her living room collecting objects: candles, a lighter, a portable tape deck. She carried these things into the bathroom. The bathroom door closed.

Tom heard her filling the bathtub. The tape deck played Motown. He sat on the couch with his legs pulled up to his chest as the Anxiety Monster's fingers ripped splinters from the door. It started throwing its weight against the door. The hinges came away from the wall. The Monster slammed into the door again. The door-hinge screws were three-quarters out. Tom was overwhelmed. He fainted.

When he woke up, two hours later, the Perfectionist was playing solitaire. She looked over at him. She smiled. She looked back at the cards.

'Feel better?' she asked.

He did. There was no sign of the Anxiety Monster.

'What happened?' he asked her.

'It left,' she said. She moved a black nine onto a red ten.

'It just left?'

'There are two ways to get rid of an anxiety monster, my friend – you either have a bath or a nap.'

Tom watches an airplane take off. The Perfectionist has finally boarded. He remembers asking the Amphibian about all the monsters.

'I don't remember a single monster before I met you,' he'd told the Amphibian. 'Now they seem to be all over the place.'

'You mean there wasn't anything you were afraid of?' the Amphibian had asked him.

'Lots.'

'What did they look like?'

It was a funny question.

'They didn't look like anything. They were ideas,' Tom told him. 'Like not being able to pay rent, or being lonely.'

'That's the most terrifying thing I've ever heard,' the Amphibian replied.

Tom picks up his carry-on luggage. He shows his ID and pass. He boards flight AC117 to Vancouver.

SIX

TAKE-OFF

Tom lowers his arms to his sides after safely stowing his carry-on luggage in the overhead compartment. He looks at the man in the aisle seat of Row 27.

'Um,' Tom says, pointing to the middle seat.

The man reluctantly angles his legs to the right. Tom squeezes past. He sits next to the Perfectionist, who has the window seat.

The Perfectionist studies two men in orange coveralls throwing luggage onto a conveyor belt. The conveyor belt carries luggage into the airplane. She doesn't feel Tom put his hand over hers. Her arm begins jerking up and down like she's being electrocuted. Tom pulls his hand away.

38

The Perfectionist wishes her arm would stop doing that.

She keeps watching the men toss luggage. She is having one of those days where everyone she sees looks like someone she used to know. The man currently tossing a red-framed knapsack onto the conveyor belt is the spitting image of an old boyfriend, Loudmotorcycle.

No one noticed W. P. Martin until he leaned too heavily on his motorcycle. He was trying to look cool in the parking lot of a 7-Eleven. It was 11:30 at night and the parking lot was full of teenagers. The bike tipped over. W. P. struggled to remain standing. The bike hit the sidewalk and the muffler was knocked off.

The teenagers started laughing. They stood around, laughing, watching W. P. push his bike upright. Nothing but the muffler seemed to be damaged. W. P. straddled the bike, turned the key, pushed his foot down and the mufflerless motorcycle roared to life.

W. P. Martin was dead – Loudmotorcycle was born. No one could ignore him now.

Loudmotorcycle covered his arms with tattoos. He rode through narrow side streets late at night, gunning the engine and setting off car alarms.

The Perfectionist met Loudmotorcycle at the fairgrounds. With three pitches he won a stretched Pepsi bottle and her heart. The Perfectionist linked her fingers through his belt-loops and he raced her through the city. She still has the hearing loss to prove it.

Then one night, a Wednesday, Loudmotorcycle swerved. A cat was sitting in the middle of the road, using its green eyes to stare at him. The cat survived. Loudmotorcycle hadn't actually come that close to it. Still, his hands trembled as he pulled the key out of the ignition. The cat kept watching.

Sitting on the grass, looking at his bike, he listened to the city. Loudmotorcycle couldn't believe how loud it all was. Even at this time of night there were sirens and traffic and a vague industrial hum. Loudmotorcycle started to wonder what he was doing with his life.

The Perfectionist dumped him. It wasn't because he never rode his motorcycle any more. It wasn't because his tattoos suddenly looked stupid. It was his insomnia. Every night, all night, he tossed and turned. Loudmotorcycle tried prescription medications, non-prescription drugs, herbal remedies, soothing music and earplugs – nothing worked. He hasn't been able to sleep since the day he swerved. Every night he lies in his bed, kept awake by city noise, wishing he'd killed that fucking cat.

The Perfectionist continues looking out the window. She sees a two-tone beige suitcase hit the conveyor belt. This is the last piece of luggage. There is nothing more to toss. The two men climb into a modified golf cart. The one driving looks exactly like her ex-boyfriend the Spooner.

Every night it'll just hit the Spooner but he can't

predict when. Sometimes he'll be asleep and it'll wake him up. Other times he'll still be reading or watching television. Every night the address is different. Sometimes it's close enough to walk. Some nights he takes the bus. Some nights, a cab.

He can visualize it long before he gets there. If it's a house or an apartment, or some strange basement room you get to from around the back, the Spooner always knows. He always finds the door unlocked, or at least unlocked to him. He never stumbles, never trips over a chair or a coffee table, as he navigates this unknown space in the dark.

The Spooner always knows where the bedroom is. Someone sleeping alone in the fetal position always occupies the bed. He gets under the covers. He holds them. They never wake up. They always whisper 'Thank you' in their sleep.

One night the Spooner was drawn to a familiar address. He found the door unlocked, or unlocked to him. He didn't need his superpower to locate the bedroom. The woman he found sleeping in the fetal position was the Perfectionist. He broke up with her the next day.

But this is the first time the Perfectionist has thought about the Spooner in a year and a half. She feels the plane taxi to the end of the runway. The engines hum. Her body is pushed back in her chair. She grabs both of her armrests.

She reminds herself to take deep breaths. The runway is a grey blur. The front of the plane tips up. A roaring sound comes from the wings. The angle of the plane increases. She looks to the front of the plane and it's like being at the back of a roller coaster. She grips her armrests tighter. The plane levels out. The seat belt sign flashes off. The Perfectionist relaxes her grip on the armrests.

Tom rushes to take his seat belt off. He pushes past the man in the aisle seat. He holds his left hand to his right wrist. He clenches and unclenches his fist as he half-jogs to the back of the plane.

The washroom on the left is unoccupied. Tom bolts the door behind him. The fluorescent light flickers on. He rolls up his sleeve and looks down at four crescent-moon cuts on his wrist. He turns on the tap and runs cold water over his wrist. The bleeding isn't bad. A mirror hangs over the stainless steel washbasin and Tom smiles at his reflection. He laughs out loud.

'She touched me,' he says. 'She touched me!'

SEVEN

THE SUPERHEROES OF TORONTO

There are 249 superheroes in the city of Toronto, Ontario, Canada. None of them have secret identities. Very few wear costumes. Most of their powers don't result in material gain. The Amphibian can survive both on land and underwater, but really, what use is that? Who's going to give him a job for that? He works as a bike courier for a company downtown called Speedy.

Even the Clock, the only superhero who can travel in time, doesn't think her power is anything special. She's quick to point out that everyone can travel in time and everybody's constantly doing it: a real superpower would be the ability not to travel in time.

There are no supervillains. Not one of the superheroes believes this. Every superhero considers one of the others a supervillian. The Perfectionist fights with the Projectionist. Businessman and the Union consider each other evil. Even the Amphibian has come to blows with the Linear.

At parties, the host will inevitably have to listen to some outraged superhero say, 'I can't believe you invited so-and-so.' Or this superhero and that superhero will run into each other on their way to the bathroom and stand there with their fingers pointing, yelling, 'Evil! Evil!!'

The Stress Bunny throws the best parties. The Amphibian took Tom to one of the Stress Bunny's end-of-summer parties. It was the first superhero party Tom was ever at. He nudged the Amphibian with his shoulder.

'Watch this,' he said to the Amphibian. 'Hey ... hey, The!' Tom called.

The Scenester looked. The Greenlighter looked. The Phoney, the Verb, the Minimalist – almost everybody in the room looked. Including the Perfectionist.

The Amphibian didn't think it was funny but the Perfectionist giggled. She'd never noticed how many of their first names were 'The'. She smiled at Tom. She flipped her hair over her shoulder.

Hypno thought the joke was funny but he didn't think his girlfriend finding it funny was funny. He hypnotized everybody in the room to forget Tom's name. He tried to hypnotize Tom into wanting to go home and discovered that he couldn't – Tom is the only person Hypno has never been able to hypnotize.

Even though she couldn't remember his name, the Perfectionist still spent the whole night talking with him.

'What's your name again?' she kept asking him.

'It's Tom,' Tom kept saying.

'Right. That's right,' she'd say. She'd immediately forget it. She forgot Tom's name eighteen times over the course of the evening.

THE FROG-KISSER

The Frog-Kisser was in high school when she first discovered her power. Dating the captain of the football team had left her drained and unfulfilled. That's when she discovered Brian, the head of the debating club, and her latent powers emerged.

Blessed with the ability to transform geeks into winners, she is cursed with the reality that once she enables this transformation, the origin of her initial attraction is gone.

FIFTH BUSINESS

Fifth Business picks a new subject every three years. His current subject could be you and you wouldn't even know it. Fifth Business is invisible.

If you are his subject he's spent the last three years watching you bathe, dress, cook, fight, caress and have moments of doubt. He's made notes while watching you watch TV, brush your teeth, burst into tears, get hired, fired and tired.

He knows everything about you. He knows the one thing that needs to happen so you can fulfill your dreams. He knows the single event that would trigger your downfall. And he's deciding, right now, which one he'll make happen.

THE SEEKER

The Seeker knows how to get anywhere from any place, even if he's never been there before. But since this is his superpower and he defines himself through it, the Seeker gets quite upset and fidgety whenever he reaches a destination. He has to immediately turn around and head somewhere else.

THE PROJECTIONIST

The Projectionist can make you believe whatever she believes. If she believes interest rates are going to fall, and you have a short conversation with the Projectionist, you will too. If she believes that, no, in fact, you didn't signal when you turned left, causing the Projectionist to ram her car into the back of yours, so will you.

Her downfall began when she fell in love with the Inverse. She absolutely, 100% fell in love with the Inverse. She projected all this emotion onto him but the Inverse, being the Inverse, simply reflected the opposite of everything she was sending.

Strangely, neither the Inverse nor the Projectionist can let go of the relationship.

THE CHIP

Chip was born with a chip on her shoulder. It's an immensely heavy chip, a chip that weighs so much it forced her to develop superhuman strength. But the chip on Chip's shoulder weighs so much that only her super-strength could remove it, but she can't use her super-strength until she gets rid of the chip and she can't get rid of the chip without using her super-strength. She appears no stronger than any regular.

EIGHT

THE FIRST NIGHT OF INVISIBILITY

For three hours and forty-five minutes the Perfectionist stares at clouds. Tom stares at the Perfectionist. Now that she's fallen asleep, Tom examines the cheese sandwich the airhostess handed him over the Prairies. Just east of the Rockies, Tom unwraps it and takes a bite. The bread tastes like plastic wrap. He sets the sandwich on the corner of his tray.

The Perfectionist snores (perfectly). Tom knows he could nudge her and the snoring would stop. It's what he used to do. But since he turned invisible Tom won't touch the Perfectionist when she's sleeping. He's only tried it once, the first night they were married – the night he thought he'd killed her.

He'd watched her step out of her wedding dress like it was a pile of snow. She left it on the floor and climbed directly under the covers. Since the reception she'd sneezed, or hiccuped, or flailed her arms each time he'd touched her. He didn't want her to do any of that but it was his wedding night and he didn't want to sleep alone. He waited until she fell asleep and held her from behind. They spooned. He fell asleep holding her.

Two hours later Tom woke up. The Perfectionist wasn't breathing. He watched her chest. Seconds passed. Finally she took a breath. Tom wasn't relieved; the breath was so deep her whole body expanded. Her feet came off the bed, her chest ballooned and her fists curled into balls. Ten seconds passed before her next one.

Tom picked her up by the shoulders. He shook her. She didn't wake up. He counted twenty seconds and still no breath.

'Wake up!' he shouted. 'Perf – wake up!' She didn't wake up.

Tom jumped off the bed. He ran into the kitchen. He phoned the Amphibian to get Hypno's number. He bit the inside of his cheek as he dialled. He cursed the day she'd met Hypno with each number he punched.

The thing is, the Perfectionist really did have the best sex of her life for the three months she dated Hypno. Then one morning, a Wednesday, she came like never before. Her toes curled. Her fingernails dug into his back.

His cock was something she never wanted to let out of her, but she realized she didn't much like the rest of him.

Hypno held her and fell asleep. She had two hours before her shift at the diner. She delicately lifted Hypno's hand, showered and changed. She gathered her toothbrush, the clothes she had in the third drawer of his dresser, the few things that hung in his closet, and the miscellaneous CDs and books. All these things fit in three white plastic grocery bags. She didn't leave a note. She just left.

When Hypno woke that morning, she was gone. He knew she wasn't coming back. He was devastated. He couldn't go to work. He couldn't eat. His cat disappeared. The only way he survived the experience was by hypnotizing himself. He dangled a watch, stared at the mirror and repeated after himself. The Perfectionist became invisible to him, a spell he broke only to attend her wedding.

Tom held the receiver close to his ear. He listened to the phone ring three times.

'Hello?' Hypno answered.

'It's Tom.'

'So?' Hypno said.

'Don't,' Tom said. 'I think I've killed her.'

'While she was sleeping?' Hypno asked.

'Yes.'

'You touched her while she was asleep?'

'I held her.'

'You shouldn't do that.'

'It's our wedding night,' Tom said.

'You can't do that.'

'What should I do?'

'She's still sleeping?'

'You'd better hope so.'

'She's fine,' Hypno assured. 'Go back and check on her, and you'll see. She's fine.'

Tom dropped the phone. He ran to the bedroom. The Perfectionist was sleeping (perfectly). Tom watched her to make sure. He sat at the foot of the bed. Ten minutes passed and her breathing was easy and regular.

Tom got off the bed still watching the Perfectionist. He stepped on her wedding dress, then picked it up, searched around and found a wooden hanger. The dress rustled as he hung it up. It took up almost half the space in the closet. He walked back to the kitchen and saw the phone on the floor. Tom picked up the receiver.

'Hello?' Tom asked into it.

'She's fine, right?' asked Hypno.

'How do I make it stop?'

'It's pretty simple.'

'Tell me!'

'Are you that afraid of her, Tom?'

'What are you talking about?'

'If you can't figure this one out, you don't deserve her.

You really don't,' Hypno said. He hung up.

Tom listened to the dial tone. He held the receiver away from his head and looked at it. He threw the phone. The receiver was skidding across the floor as the Perfectionist walked into the kitchen. She stepped over it without looking down, went to the sink and filled a glass with water. She sat at the kitchen table, staring straight ahead.

'See me!' Tom screamed. He waved his hands in front of her face. He pushed the kitchen table away. The Perfectionist reached down. She took hold of a glass that wasn't there, raised her arm and drank from her empty hand.

Tom opened a cupboard. He took out a dinner plate. Raising it over his head, Tom let it fall. The plate shattered.

The Perfectionist didn't look up.

Tom dropped another plate. The Perfectionist stared at the wall in front of her. Tom threw a plate into the wall she stared at. The Perfectionist didn't look up. Tom reached to the back of the cupboard. He stacked all the remaining plates.

'Look at me!' he screamed. He lifted the stack over his head and his housecoat bunched up under his arms.

The Perfectionist didn't look at him.

Tom dropped the plates. They hit the floor and shattered into countless bits. The Perfectionist got up from the kitchen table and set her imaginary glass in the sink. She stepped on the bits of broken plate and cut her feet to ribbons. She didn't say a word. She tracked blood all the way to the bedroom.

Tom discovered that touching her feet made her seasick. The Perfectionist threw up into a bowl as he pulled slivers of china out of her feet. He washed her feet. He bandaged them and slept on the floor.

In seat F27 the Perfectionist continues snoring. Tom puts his head in his hands. He leans forward, reaches into the pocket of the seat in front of him and pulls the plastic off a pair of headphones. He plugs them in. The last passenger left the volume at nine and opera plays so loud he can hear it with the headphones still on his lap.

Tom looks at the headphones. He can hear the music, but he can't see it. 'If music is invisible, can being invisible be all bad?' Tom thinks to himself.

Tom unplugs the headphones. He puts them back into the pocket of the seat in front of him.

NINE

SIX HUNDRED CIGARETTES LATER

One morning exactly five months after their wedding, the Perfectionist woke up even earlier than usual. She walked to her corner store to buy a package of cigarettes but when she got to the counter she hesitated. She asked for three cartons of cigarettes and bought a pink disposable lighter as well. From the corner store she walked to a thrift store where for $3.99 she bought the largest ashtray they had.

In the same plastic bag she carried the cigarettes, the ashtray and the pink plastic lighter back to the apartment. She upended the plastic bag on the kitchen table, the ashtray wobbling as it hit the tabletop.

Using a letter opener she unwrapped the three cartons of cigarettes. She took the plastic covering off the twenty-four packages. She took all the cigarettes out of their packages and made a stack of 600 cigarettes.

The Perfectionist started smoking. Six hundred seemed like an incredible number of cigarettes to her. She was sure Tom would return before she smoked the last one.

Twelve days later the 600th cigarette was between her nicotine-stained fingers. The plastic pink lighter was slippery in her hand. Her thumb flicked. She pushed the flame into the tip of the cigarette. She inhaled, didn't cough, and somebody knocked on her door.

The Perfectionist exhaled. She set the lit cigarette on the edge of the ashtray. On the way to the door her inner voice said not to open it. 'He wouldn't knock,' it told her. She opened the door anyway.

The man who stood in front of her was tall. His hair was freshly cut and greying at the temples. His black suit, white shirt and black tie were pressed. His shoes shone. Beside him on the sidewalk was a sample case big enough to hold a vacuum cleaner. He smiled at the Perfectionist.

The Perfectionist has always hated vacuum salesmen. There's no reason, no traumatic episode in her past, no ex-lover or absent father who is one. She just doesn't like them.

'I don't want a vacuum,' the Perfectionist said.

'I'm not selling vacuums,' he answered. His voice was lyrical, calm and reassuring.

'What are you selling?' the Perfectionist asked.

'I'm selling love,' he answered.

The Perfectionist leaned against the door jamb. The smell of cigarettes came from her hair and her clothes. She backed out of the doorway and he followed her inside.

In the kitchen he set down his sample case. He tugged up his trouser legs as he sat. He crossed his right leg over his left, revealing argyle socks.

'What kind of love are we interested in today?' he asked.

'What kinds do you have?'

'Well,' he said. He stood up. 'I've got the love you want, the love you think you want, the love you think you want but don't when you finally get it …'

'That must be very popular.'

'It is.'

'What else have you got?'

'I've got the love that's yours as long as you do what you're told, the love that worries it's not good enough, the love that worries it'll be found out, the love that fears being judged and found lacking, the love that's almost – but not quite – strong enough, the love that makes you feel they're better than you …'

'Stop.'

'What?'

'I don't want any of those.'

'What kind do you want?'

'I want the kind I had with Tom.'

'And what kind was that?'

'It was true love,' the Perfectionist said.

She locked eyes with the salesman. He swallowed. It made his eyes look sad.

'Then you'll need one of these,' he replied. His eyes didn't look sad any more. They sparkled. He dipped to his right, picked up his sample case, lifted it as high as he could and slammed it onto the kitchen table. He snapped the left clasp open. He snapped the right clasp open. He flipped open the lid, reached in and pulled out a vacuum.

'You are a vacuum salesman?' the Perfectionist hissed.

'You don't really believe true love exists outside one of these?' he asked.

The salesman stood motionless, holding out the vacuum. The kitchen was silent. His arms got tired. He lowered the vacuum and put it back in the sample case.

'Thank you for your time,' the Perfectionist said. She took his card and gently escorted him to the front door of the apartment.

The Perfectionist returned to the kitchen and noticed her lit cigarette in the ashtray. It was half-burnt. She reached out and extinguished it. She flipped through the yellow pages and phoned the first travel agency she saw. She purchased a one-way ticket to Vancouver.

TEN

TASKS #5 TO #7

The Perfectionist wakes up. She watches clouds and mentally rechecks her 'Things To Do Before Leaving' list. Tasks #5 to #7 were all 'call sister' (#4 final mop and wax; #8 call airport to check for a flight delay). The Perfectionist replays these phone conversations in her mind. The first call (#5) was to her eldest sister, the Face.

The Face was eight years old when she first noticed how photographs taken of her were slightly out of focus. When the Face looked in mirrors, even if she kept very still, her reflection was always blurry. During high school she was very popular but she had no close friends.

After high school the Face studied at the Nova Scotia

College of Art and Design in Halifax, Nova Scotia. In painting class the first assignment was a self-portrait. Holding her brush, the Face studied her classmates. They mixed colours and applied thick brushstrokes to the canvas. The Face's brush was still. She didn't know how to begin.

That night she phoned three of her classmates and asked them to describe what she looked like. They all responded that she was the most beautiful woman they'd ever seen. But when she asked for details, they couldn't provide any. They couldn't tell her what colour her eyes were. They didn't know if her teeth were straight, or if her hair was wavy, or if her lips were thick. They only knew she was the most beautiful woman they'd ever seen.

The Face submitted a blank canvas and got an A+. Everyone agreed it was the most beautiful self-portrait they'd ever seen and it looked exactly like her. That afternoon she started sewing a hood. She finished it the following Wednesday. She hasn't taken it off in seventeen years.

The Face wasn't home. The Perfectionist had planned this. She left a message apologizing for missing her and a promise that she'd call as soon as she landed in Vancouver.

The Perfectionist went on to task #6. She called her other older sister, the Elongating Woman, who was named Donna at birth. On Donna's eighteenth birthday her boyfriend was the passenger in a Toyota Corolla that was t-boned by a pickup truck. He died on his way to the hospital and for the next three years all Donna could think about was timing. What if he'd stopped for something? What if they'd hit a red light? What if he'd gotten into that car ten seconds later? It seemed like such a simple thing, so easy to change, and she started believing she could change it. All she had to do was reach back into time and delay him, so she stretched out her arms.

She stretched her arms down Queen Street, past people and streetcars. She stretched her arms onto the Gardiner Expressway. She stretched her arms faster than highway traffic. She stretched and stretched and stretched but she was only able to put her arms around the city. She couldn't reach back in time and she's never forgiven herself.

The Elongating Woman answered her phone.

'It's me,' the Perfectionist said.

'Don't go,' said the Elongating Woman.

'I can't wait any longer,' the Perfectionist said. 'There are limits.'

'I know,' the Elongating Woman said. 'I know that.'

The Perfectionist promised to call the moment she landed in Vancouver. She hung up the phone and called her younger sister, the Ticker (task #7).

The Ticker is a quiet superhero who makes everyone nervous. Her superpower is her amazing potential. Sitting at the edge of parties, responding to inquiries but never starting them, the Ticker is always watching and waiting – as is everybody else.

Certainly she could do anything she wanted to, but what would that anything be? Brilliant art? Mass crime? World peace or medical school? And will she ever do it? Not even the Ticker knows. She answered her phone on the first ring.

'I'll miss ya,' said the Ticker.

'I'll miss you too,' said the Perfectionist.

'Perf?' asked the Ticker. Her voice made the Perfectionist nervous. The Ticker rarely sounded this serious.

'Yes?' asked the Perfectionist.

'Why am I not working out?'

'You will. I know you will,' the Perfectionist said. There was a silence.

'Okay,' the Ticker said.

'I should get going,' the Perfectionist said.

'I'll let you go then.'

'Okay.'

They both hung up.

The Perfectionist replays this last conversation and worries that she rushed her sister off the phone. She worries about all of them. She puts her finger on the airplane window and draws a circle. Her sisters, the Perfectionist concludes, are perfectly sad. She feels lucky to have escaped the tragedies that happened to them. Then the Perfectionist remembers her wedding. She remembers the six months since. She remembers why she's flying to Vancouver.

ELEVEN

THE TWO BOXES

Tom has returned to the toilet on the airplane. He's in the one on the right. Three people have knocked. He puts his fingers underneath his eyes and pulls down the skin. He studies his eyes, all red rims and dark circles. 'Raccoon,' he says. He's never seen himself look so tired.

This isn't true. Tom has seen himself this tired once before, but that tired was so different from this tired. He can remember everything about that tired; the television was still on, the only light in the living room, and it flickered blue like a strobe light.

The Perfectionist had sat up. She pulled down her shirt. Her hair was messed up (perfectly). She studied

63

him. She kept her eyes open and kissed him. The kiss lingered. Tom lost track of whose lips were whose. Then the Perfectionist stood up. She pointed the remote at the television and turned it off. She reached out for Tom's hand and he gave it to her.

They walked upstairs, Tom a step behind her. He tried not to stare at her ass. He squeezed her hand and wished his palm wasn't so sweaty. They reached the top of the stairs and turned towards her bedroom.

Only three days earlier they'd had their first kiss, but this wouldn't be the first time Tom had been in the Perfectionist's bedroom. One night, a Wednesday night, not even a month ago, she'd brought him upstairs. They'd both attended the Ear's birthday party, and they'd both been drinking, and they'd ended up walking home together. At her front door she'd invited Tom up. He'd accepted.

The Perfectionist hadn't been with anyone since she broke up with Hypno. The sex with him had been so good the Perfectionist had taken it for granted. She really liked Tom, was sure they'd become really great friends, but nothing more. She didn't know if their friendship would survive a one-nighter but she felt reckless and took Tom straight to her bedroom.

The Perfectionist pushed Tom onto her bed. She took off his shirt. She took off his shoes and his socks. She took off his pants. She took off his boxers.

With most guys the Perfectionist would stop there. She didn't. She was still feeling reckless. She took off his skin. She took off his nervous system. She lifted up his rib cage. His heart beat in her hand. And there, underneath it, she found a jewelled golden box. She opened it. Inside she found his hopes, his dreams and his fears. She stared at them. She was surprised to find them there and surprised at how beautiful they were. At that exact moment, the Perfectionist fell in love with Tom.

She put back the box and his skin and his clothes. She held him.

The Perfectionist remembered that moment as they approached her bedroom door. Tom slowed down. The Perfectionist didn't. She walked past her bedroom. She kept walking.

There was a room at the very end of the hallway. Tom hadn't noticed it before. The door was closed. The Perfectionist let go of his hand. She opened the door and flicked on the light. Inside, the carpet was worn and grey. Finishing nails stuck out of white drywall. In the centre of the room were two giant cardboard boxes, the kind refrigerators come packed in.

On the box to the left, in the Perfectionist's handwriting, was the word 'FRIEND'. On the box to the right, also in the Perfectionist's handwriting, was the word 'LOVER'. These two boxes were the only objects in the room.

Tom looked at the Perfectionist. The Perfectionist

looked at him. Tom looked back to the boxes and then back at the Perfectionist. He scratched his head.

'Well?' the Perfectionist asked.

Tom looked at her, looked at the boxes and looked back at the Perfectionist. He still didn't understand.

'Which one?' she demanded. She moved her arms, suggesting he should get in one.

Tom walked into the room and stood between the two boxes. He looked at the one marked 'LOVER' and he looked at the one marked 'FRIEND'. He made his decision quickly. With sharp steps he moved in front of the box marked 'FRIEND'. Picking it up, he lifted it over his head and put it inside the box marked 'LOVER'. Then he turned around, picked up the Perfectionist, and lifted her inside the boxes. He climbed in with her. In the morning, there wasn't much left of either box.

Tom runs his finger along the stainless-steel tap above the sink. With a little water he pats down his hair. He puts fresh toilet paper on the cuts on his wrist before unbolting the bathroom door. The 'occupied' light switches off.

TWELVE

FIND YOUR OWN SUPERHERO NAME

It's true most superheroes have funny names. But they have to come up with these names by themselves. Think about how hard it is. Try it, right now; boil down your personality and abilities to a single phrase or image. If you can do that, you're probably a superhero already.

Part of the problem with finding your superhero name is that it may refer to something you don't like about yourself. It may actually be the part of yourself you hate the most, would pay money to get rid of. Certainly the Perfectionist had a hard time coming to terms with her superpower. The Gambler, One Night and Brutally Honest all spent years accepting their superpowers.

The final stage of finding your superhero name is accepting how little difference it really makes. Okay, there's this thing you can do, a thing you can do like no other person on the planet. That makes you special, but being special really doesn't mean anything. You still have to get dressed in the morning. Your shoelaces still break. Your lover will still leave you if you don't treat her right.

THE SLOTH

The Sloth hated himself. He considered himself lazy. He had a dead-end job and no plans to get a better one. His relationship was on-again-off-again, and he never got to the gym even though he kept paying the membership dues.

There was mould in his refrigerator and he watched reruns on TV. Sometimes he wore the same pair of socks twice in the same week.

The Sloth would sit on his couch, paralyzed by all the things he wasn't taking care of. Then one day, a Wednesday, he just said, 'Fuck it!' He threw his hands up into the air and said, 'Fuck it!' This was the day that the Sloth discovered his superpower, an amazing ability to say 'Fuck it' and really, truly mean it.

WILD MOOD SWINGER

One of the few superheroes to wear a costume, Wild Mood Swinger is never seen without his large-lapelled polyester plaid leisure suit with white shoes and a matching belt. Blessed with the ability to achieve the highest emotional heights and cursed with the ability to sink to the lowest emotional depths, Wild Mood Swinger often does so during the same conversation. Strangely attractive to women.

COPYCAT

Copycat has the ability to mimic anyone's personal style. Which wouldn't be so bad, perhaps even be a compliment, if she wasn't able to perfect her subjects' style to the point where they start looking like less successful versions of themselves.

THE INVERSE

Shake the Inverse's hand and the exact opposite of your life will flash before your eyes. This can be so overwhelming that the Inverse will not shake your hand unless you ask him to, and sometimes not even then.

A case in point is Businessman. When the Inverse shook Businessman's hand, Businessman saw himself as having a work and going to life. The experience was so intense that Businessman retired the next day.

It's exactly that sort of responsibility that the Inverse seeks to avoid and it's why he has never shaken his own hand.

MR OPPORTUNITY

He knocks on doors and stands there. You'd be surprised how few doors get answered.

MISTRESS CLEANASYOUGO

The most powerful superhero of all, the one everyone wishes they were, is Mistress Cleanasyougo. At the end of every day she folds her clothes. She never leaves scissors on the table, pens with no ink are thrown in the trash, wet towels are always hung up, dishes are washed directly after dinner and nothing is left unsaid.

THIRTEEN

BEGINNING DESCENT

The captain's voice comes through Tom's headphones. In confident tones he announces that flight AC117 is commencing its descent. They will be arriving in Vancouver in twenty minutes. Local time will be 5:17 p.m. The captain requests that all passengers return to their seats and fasten their seat belts. Tom looks up. None of the passengers are standing so no one moves. He feels the plane tilt downwards. He tries not to cry. He has twenty minutes to convince his wife that he isn't invisible. He disobeys the captain's orders and dares another trip to the bathroom. He pushes past the man in seat 27D.

As Tom walks down the aisle, the man in seat 27D

begins to study the Perfectionist. He watches her watch clouds out the airplane window. The Perfectionist notices she's being studied. She doesn't look over. She keeps her eyes on the clouds.

He swallows, clears his throat. His thumb and forefinger rub together.

'Perf?' he asks.

The Perfectionist looks over. He's looking right at her. For the first time she looks right at him. She reaches out and traces her index finger across his lips.

'Literal?' she asks.

'Literal?' says the Broken-Hearted Man. 'Nobody's called me that in years.'

The Literal and the Perfectionist dated in high school. They were very much in love. They were each other's first. They separated to go to university but pledged to stay together.

To prove his love the Literal gave the Perfectionist his heart. He put it in a shoebox, wrapped the box in silver paper and carried it down to the post office. After licking twenty-nine dollars and forty-seven cents' worth of stamps, he addressed the package to the Perfectionist, c/o McGill University, Montreal, Quebec.

Three weeks later, the same shoebox arrived in the Literal's mailbox. It was wrapped in the same silver paper, but the box had been opened. His heart was inside. At that moment, the Literal stopped being the Literal. He became the Broken-Hearted Man. He was so crushed he never talked to her again.

'What are the chances I'd be sitting next to her on an airplane?' the Broken-Hearted Man asks himself. Impossible odds. Must be fate. Daily for thirteen years, sometimes three times a day, he'd rehearsed this moment. He knew exactly what he was going to say, what tone of voice he'd use. He wouldn't be bitter – that would make him look weak. He'd be casual. He would be glad to see her. It wouldn't be the most important moment of his day.

'It's been so long,' the Perfectionist says.

All the Broken-Hearted Man's plans evaporate. His eyes go wide. He can't stop it. He can't spin it or control it. It simply floods out of him.

'Why did you do that?' he wails. 'Why would you do that to me? Why did you return my heart?'

The Perfectionist stares at the Broken-Hearted Man. Her teeth grind together.

'I loved you so much,' the Perfectionist says. Her eyes have gone glossy. 'Without it, what would you have loved me with?'

The Broken-Hearted Man says nothing. He looks at his shoes and nods. He moves to the back of the airplane, finds an empty seat.

Tom returns from the washroom. He sees the Perfectionist crying. He strokes her hair with his hand. He almost feels her lean into him. She doesn't hiccup.

FOURTEEN

THE BUTTON FACTORY GALLERY

Tom watches the Perfectionist sniff. In the washroom he'd realized that smell, like sound, was invisible. He scrubbed the deodorant from his underarms. He ran on the spot as fast as he could for six minutes. He's still out of breath. Sweat drips from his forehead. There are moisture stains under his arms.

The Perfectionist leans towards him. She sniffs. He unbuttons the top three buttons of his shirt and holds it open at the collar. The Perfectionist leans closer. Tom flaps his arms like a chicken. She closes her eyes. She breathes in until her lungs are full.

'Who are you fighting?' Tom asks. A good question,

but Tom's referring to a specific experience they had at the Projectionist's art show at the Button Factory Gallery.

Tom and the Perfectionist both received an invitation.

He'd assumed she wouldn't want to go but he was wrong. She wanted to see what the Projectionist called art. The Projectionist is the only superhero ever to receive a Canada Council grant.

The reception started at seven and Tom and the Perfectionist stepped from their cab at nine. They entered the gallery. It was shoulder to shoulder with superheroes. Everybody was there: the Cartographer, 360, Fifteenminutesago, the Barometer, even the Scenester.

Tom and the Perfectionist circulated through the hot room. The Perfectionist was sweating (perfectly). The white walls of the gallery were bare – they couldn't find any art. The room held nothing but superheroes. At 9:15 p.m they were ready to leave. The Amphibian caught them on their way out the door.

'Fantastic, isn't it?' asked the Amphibian. He held a large glass of wine in his hand. Stains on the rim showed it'd been filled several times.

Tom rolled his eyes. The Perfectionist crossed her arms.

'About as expected,' she said.

'You didn't go into the back room, did you?' the Amphibian asked.

'There's a back room?' asked Tom.

'Follow me,' the Amphibian said. He pushed through

the superheroes. Tom and the Perfectionist followed.

At the far end of the room was a tiny door. The Amphibian got on his hands and knees. He crawled through the door.

'I don't want to get my trousers dirty,' said Tom.

'I've got to see this,' said the Perfectionist. She crawled through the tiny door. Tom followed her (and looked up her skirt).

The room on the other side was bigger than the one they'd just left. A mirror covered the far wall completely. It looked like a regular mirror. Tom, the Perfectionist and the Amphibian stood in front of it. Their reflections weren't distorted in any way.

Tom rolled his eyes. The Perfectionist crossed her arms. They were both disappointed, a sentiment Tom was about to express when his reflection leapt out of the mirror and started running towards him. The Perfectionist's reflection jumped out of the mirror and started running towards her. So did the Amphibian's.

With his reflection running towards him, Tom didn't know what to do. He raised his fists. His reflection raised its fists. They sized each other up. They circled around each other.

Tom found an opening. He jabbed with a right, which his reflection blocked with a left. His reflection threw a right hook, which Tom blocked with his left arm. In his peripheral vision Tom saw the Perfectionist fighting the same fight.

Tom's arms began to ache. His knuckles were bleeding. Bruises were forming on his forearms. He couldn't keep this up much longer, and his reflection showed no signs of tiring.

'What are you guys doing?' yelled the Amphibian.

The Amphibian's voice surprised Tom. Tom hadn't been this surprised by the Amphibian since the day he'd taken him to see the Salzburg Chamber Orchestra perform Mozart's Serenades Nos. 3 and 4.

Tom had wanted the Amphibian to see everything. The Amphibian had never been to a classical music concert before. They were the third and fourth in their seats. A half-hour later the orchestra came out. Some of the musicians played scales. Others simply tuned their instruments. Some played the same three or four bars over and over again. The musicians finished tuning and the house lights dimmed. The conductor walked into view.

The Amphibian stood up. His clapping was frantic.

'That was fantastic!' he screamed. The rest of the evening just disappointed him.

Just like his friends were disappointing him now.

'What are you doing?' the Amphibian repeated. His voice was filled with disbelief. It made Tom and the Perfectionist stop. When they stopped, their reflections stopped. All four turned and looked at the Amphibian, who was sitting on the floor across from his reflection.

The two Amphibians were sharing the same glass of wine. They both looked annoyed.

'These are friends of yours?' asked the Amphibian on the right.

'Two of the best I have,' answered the Amphibian on the left. They rolled their eyes and continued their conversation.

The airhostess comes around and collects Tom's headphones. Tom hands them over. He turns towards the Perfectionist, leans in close.

'I know you're fighting yourself,' Tom says. 'I know you want to see me.' But the Perfectionist keeps staring out the window of the airplane.

FIFTEEN

TENSE

The Perfectionist continues smelling Tom. It's his post-exercise smell. She looks at her watch. She has thirteen minutes before the plane lands. She needs to talk to the Clock. Putting her tray in the upright position, she settles back in her chair, closes her eyes and falls asleep.

The Perfectionist's eyeballs flicker behind her eyelids. Even though she and the Clock both live in Toronto, and it's not even a ten-dollar cab ride between their houses, they never manage to find the time to get together. So, at least twice a month, the Clock visits the Perfectionist in her dreams.

They sit in matching yellow mesh lawn chairs. The

strapping pinches the Perfectionist's left thigh. She shifts in her chair, looks over her shoulder and sees the cottage her family rented every summer until she was eighteen. She wiggles dry sand between her toes. It's 3:30 in the afternoon. She hopes she's wearing sunscreen and sniffs the air.

'Can you smell that?' the Perfectionist asks the Clock.

'Smell what?'

'Tom.'

'Only if Tom smells like dead fish,' answers the Clock.

'I swear I can smell Tom,' she says, folding her hands in her lap. She looks at her fingers. Her nails are never bitten here. 'What's it like?' she asks the Clock.

'What's what like?'

'Travelling. Being able to travel to the future.'

'It's nothing like you think,' the Clock tells her.

'Will you take me?'

'You wouldn't like it.'

'I just want to see it.'

'It's not like you're imagining.'

'Take me there,' the Perfectionist pleads. She puts her hand on the Clock's arm. 'I really need to see it.'

Part of the reason the Perfectionist is so desperate to see the future is that she once got stuck in the present. She had a fling with Terry Cloth, whose superpower is the ability to make every day feel like Sunday. They met on February 11th and spent the next five months in bed.

They didn't have a lot of sex; they moved the TV into the bedroom. They ordered in and had supplies delivered. They started screening their calls and then stopped answering the phone altogether. June went by and neither of them had left the apartment.

Then one morning, the Perfectionist woke up early. She let Terry Cloth sleep. Puttering around in the bathroom, she stepped on the scale and waited for the needle to stop swinging back and forth. When it did she was so shocked she jumped off the scale, spilling red wine on her white housecoat.

She'd gained fifteen pounds. All her clothes were too tight and her housecoat was the only article of clothing she felt comfortable in. The washing machine was broken. She pulled on a pair of Terry's track pants and a white T-shirt that stretched over her belly. She carried her housecoat down two flights of stairs to the street.

Outside she sniffed in the fresh air. The sound of traffic was overwhelming. There were so many people. She walked to the laundromat, watching the sidewalk.

The wash cycle was twenty-seven minutes long. The Perfectionist read a newspaper, had a coffee and eavesdropped on people talking about their jobs. She looked at her watch; it didn't feel like Sunday any more. It felt like Wednesday. It was Wednesday.

The Perfectionist knew Wednesdays weren't as good as Sundays. But it still felt good to have one. She never went back to Terry Cloth.

Terry Cloth was heartbroken. His superpower so often went unrecognized and he thought he'd found someone who really appreciated him. His life became an endless series of Sunday afternoons, instead of Sunday mornings, until he hooked up with Mr Breakfast.

The Clock pushes her sunglasses on top of her head. 'You want to go because of Tom?' she asks.

'Yes.'

'Then what I'm about to show you will only disappoint you,' the Clock says.

'I think I know that.'

'Okay.'

The Clock picks up her lawn chair. She sets it down so her back is to the water. The meshing sags as the Clock sits face-to-face with the Perfectionist. Their knees touch. She holds the Perfectionist's chin. She tips the Perfectionist's head down until their foreheads meet.

'Close your eyes,' the Clock whispers.

'They are closed.'

'Close them.'

The Perfectionist closes her eyes. The Clock begins to hum. The hum is high-pitched and steady. It drowns out the seagulls and the surf. The Perfectionist can feel it in her chest. It keeps getting louder. It fills her ears. She can't think about anything else. Then it's gone. All sound is gone.

'We're here,' the Clock says.

The Perfectionist opens her eyes. She sees nothing. It's white. All white. There's no up. There's no down. No horizon. Nothing. It's just white.

'Clock, what is this?' asks the Perfectionist. Her voice is shaky.

'This is the future.'

'This is the future?' the Perfectionist asks. Her mouth is dry. She forces herself to swallow. 'Why is the future like this?'

'Because it hasn't happened yet,' says the Clock.

The Perfectionist wakes up. She's on the airplane. She feels the plane's descent. She flares her nostrils. She breathes, deeply. She can still smell Tom.

SIXTEEN

INVISIBILITY

Tom isn't considered invisible since his invisibility is isolated to the Perfectionist. But there are invisible superheroes, who can be divided into two groups: those who can switch from visible to invisible at will, and those who are invisible at all times. David Duncan falls into the second group. After five months of Tom's isolated invisibility, the Amphibian wrote David Duncan's phone number on a piece of paper. He gave that piece of paper to Tom.

'You should call him,' the Amphibian urged. They were drinking beer at the Diplomatico on College Street.

'Why?' Tom asked.

'Because he used to be the Blue Outcast and he's one of the few invisibles who'll talk to you.'

'What would I talk to him about?'

'Being invisible.'

'But I'm not invisible.'

'He might have, you know, a perspective. He might have advice for you.'

Tom took the number. He folded it into his wallet.

Three days later, just after the Perfectionist stopped smoking, Tom found an airline ticket to Vancouver sitting on the kitchen table. He understood the consequences and became desperate. He called David Duncan. Duncan agreed to meet him at Pauper's Pub, a fake English pub on Bloor Street.

David Duncan had come out of the womb invisible. The nurse washed away the blood and afterbirth to find nobody there. As a toddler he'd wiggle out of his diaper. His parents had to wait until he cried from hunger to find him. They almost died of worry. They took the drastic step of painting him blue.

Using a water-based non-toxic paint, they kept him painted until he was five years old. On his first day of school his parents left the decision with him. He could choose to remain blue or to return to his natural invisible state.

David went up to the bathroom. He had an hour until the school bus arrived. He filled the sink with water. He washed all the blue away and looked at himself in the mirror. Lifting his toothbrush, he watched it float through the air. It terrified him. He decided to remain blue.

David attended public school painted blue. He made no friends. He became the Blue Outcast.

All during high school the Blue Outcast resisted the temptation to sneak into the girls' changing room. Not once did he steal into a teacher's desk. He always paid to see a movie.

Graduating with average marks, the Blue Outcast got a job at a call centre and a one-bedroom apartment just east of Church Street. He led a solitary life. Every morning he would paint himself blue like other men shave. No one ever suspected he was invisible. They just thought he was weird.

Then one day, a Wednesday, the Blue Outcast worked late at the call centre. He waited for the 6:04 streetcar. Normally he got the 5:15. This is where he saw her. She was hard to miss. She was orange.

The Blue Outcast was in line for the front doors of the streetcar. The Orange Exile was exiting through the rear doors. They made brief eye contact, but nothing more.

The Blue Outcast changed his routine. He took that streetcar, the 504, at 6:04 everyday. The Blue Outcast and the Orange Exile noticed each other more and more. They made eye contact for longer periods of time. The Blue Outcast made sure to be at the end of the line for the front doors of the streetcar. The Orange Exile made sure to be first out the back doors. They began waving to each other as they passed on the street. They still hadn't chatted or exchanged names. That didn't seem to be the point.

Six weeks after they'd become aware of each other, a thunderstorm rolled across the city. The rain backed up the storm drains. Lightning struck close to the Blue Outcast's call centre. It was 7:30. He'd missed the 6:04. He was the only one in the office. The sound boomed through the room. He looked out the window to see if there was any damage.

At that exact moment, the Orange Exile was looking out the window of her apartment. The call centre and the Orange Exile's apartment were directly across from each other, on the second floors of three-storey buildings.

The Blue Outcast looked at the Orange Exile. Lightning cracked again. She put her index finger in her mouth. She pulled it out. It wasn't orange any more. It was invisible. She held it up for the Blue Outcast to see.

The Blue Outcast cried. His tears cut streaks of invisibility down his face. He stepped back from the window. He undressed. Naked, he left the call centre. He walked to the ground floor, stepped into the rain and looked across the street where orange feet and orange legs were standing in an orange puddle.

They stood in the rain. The Blue Outcast looked up at the sky and held out his arms. He let rain fall on his face. He looked down at his hands and didn't see them. He looked back across the street and couldn't see the Orange Exile.

Neither of them has been seen since.

Tom arrived at the pub ten minutes late. He searched for an empty table. He found one where a glass of beer was drinking itself and sat down.

'I'm Tom,' said Tom. Thanks for meeting me.' He held out his hand and David Duncan shook it.

'I don't know how I can help you,' David Duncan said.

'Neither do I,' said Tom. Tom didn't know where to look. He focused on a beer ad where David's voice seemed to be coming from.

'What do you want to know?'

'I want to know how to convince my wife that I'm not invisible.'

'But you're not invisible.'

'I am to her,' said Tom.

'Yeah,' David Duncan said. 'I was invisible to my wife, too.'

'Was?'

'It didn't work out.'

The waitress came over. Tom ordered a beer. He slid the ashtray between his hands. They didn't say anything. David Duncan emptied his glass.

'Sometimes these things happen for a reason,' David said.

'Yeah.'

'We're not together any more, but if I hadn't met her, I'd still be blue.'

'Yeah,' said Tom.

'Maybe you just weren't ready for it.'

'Yeah,' Tom repeated. The waitress brought his beer. Tom pushed it across the table. He pulled a twenty from his wallet, set it down and walked home.

SEVENTEEN

MINIMALIST APARTMENT

Turbulence bumps the airplane. Tom and the Perfectionist bounce as high as their seat belts let them. Tom looks at his watch. He has four minutes left. He thinks about the return portion of his ticket. He contemplates going home to the empty rooms he used to share with the Perfectionist.

In their apartment Tom and the Perfectionist had 105 articles (plus personal hygiene products). Before they moved in together, they had many more. On moving day Tom rented the largest truck U-Haul offered. The Amphibian helped him move.

'You've got a lot of stuff,' said the Amphibian. He carried a box of books. On top of the box of books were a stool and a crate of vinyl LPs.

'I don't have a lot of stuff,' Tom answered. He carried a vintage microwave oven and a rice maker.

'You have a lot of stuff,' the Amphibian repeated.

They tried to fit everything from the basement apartment into the truck. It didn't fit. The truck was full and a quarter of Tom's possessions remained behind.

Tom and the Amphibian locked the truck. They drove over to the Perfectionist's. When they arrived, they had a beer. The Perfectionist looked into the back of the truck. She reorganized. The truck was now half-empty.

The Amphibian left for ball practice. Tom and the Perfectionist started loading her possessions into the truck.

'You have a lot of stuff,' Tom told her. He was carrying a box filled with antique cookware.

'I don't have a lot of stuff,' the Perfectionist said. She carried a box filled with dresses she'd worn in high school.

Not all of the Perfectionist's possessions fit into the truck. Three-quarters did. The rest they left behind. They drove over to the new place and parked on the street. Excited, they ran inside. They were enjoying the view from the bedroom when they saw someone stealing their U-Haul.

By the time they'd finished with the police reports and convinced U-Haul to rent them a second truck, it was getting dark. Tom and the Perfectionist were tired.

Without talking, they drove to Tom's apartment. They loaded what remained. Then, still without talking, they drove to the Perfectionist's apartment and loaded what was left on her lawn. All the objects fit easily into the van.

Tom started the truck. He sighed. The Perfectionist crossed her arms. They drove downtown, towards their new apartment, past the alley where they'd encountered Sleazy Jim just after they'd started going out together.

The alley was between two stores that had been vacant for years. Sleazy Jim always stood in front of it. One Wednesday, after fighting for seventy-two consecutive hours, Tom and the Perfectionist walked past it. Sleazy Jim was waiting.

'Psssst,' Sleazy Jim said.

Tom and the Perfectionist continued walking. They ignored him, ignoring the one button holding his trench coat closed and how he smelled like a hospital. They'd ignored him a hundred times before.

'You wanna buy a myth?' Sleazy Jim added. He'd never said that before. Neither of them could ignore it. They stopped. They turned and looked at Sleazy Jim. Sleazy Jim nodded. Tom and the Perfectionist followed him.

The wind blew sheets of newspaper around. Halfway down the alley was a dumpster. They all ducked behind it. Sleazy Jim stood with his back to the brick wall. Over his right shoulder 'AC/DC RULES' was spray-painted in yellow. He unbuttoned the top and only button. He opened his trench coat. Inside, safety-pinned to the fabric, were three envelope-sized pieces of paper. On each card he'd hand-written a slogan using thick block capitals. Sleazy Jim pointed with a long, scabby finger.

'I've got "Good triumphs over evil". "All men are created equal". "Love conquers all". Whaddya want?' Sleazy Jim asked.

Tom looked at the Perfectionist. He made his 'no big deal to me' face. The Perfectionist looked at Tom. She made her 'same here' face.

'I'm sorry,' Tom said. 'We already own all of those.'

At that exact moment, Tom and the Perfectionist knew they should be together forever.

Their new apartment was another ten minutes past Sleazy Jim's alley. They drove in silence. They unloaded everything. When they were finished, they had a green armchair, a white sofa, three potted plants, a kitchen table with four chairs, four complete table settings, a skillet, two knives, three pots of various sizes, a queen-sized bed, two sets of sheets, one comforter, seven collar shirts, seven blouses, fourteen T-shirts, fourteen pairs of trousers (six jeans, eight slacks), seven sweaters, fourteen pairs of socks, fourteen pairs of underwear, personal hygiene products and four large white towels.

The plane hits another patch of turbulence. Tom puts his head in his hands. The plane continues to descend. Tom visualizes the apartment he shared with the Perfectionist. He realizes two things: the 105 items they had fit their needs perfectly, and it was the Perfectionist who made this happen.

'That's it!' Tom yells. Rows 25 through 29 turn and look at him. Tom smiles, unfastens his seat belt and leans forward.

EIGHTEEN

LANDING

The sound of the wheels extending startles the Perfectionist. She looks out the window. The glass and steel buildings of Vancouver are in the distance. She feels how steep the plane's arc is. There's a lightweight feeling in her. She puts her hand on her stomach.

The runway is in sight. The plane banks and becomes parallel with the runway. The Perfectionist looks to the right of the asphalt and sees, very tiny, the plane's shadow. Nothing more than a blob. The plane continues descending. The shadow gains more definition. It starts to grow wings. Now she can see the nose of the plane, the tail.

She swears she can smell Tom. Her eyes mist.

She can do this. As soon as the wheels touch Vancouver she'll move on. She'll make it perfect. She'll make Vancouver perfect. She has the power to do this.

'Perf,' Tom says. He watches her bend down. She slips her shoes back on. He leans down with her. The plane is four hundred feet from the ground. Tom leans very close to her ear. Three hundred feet. The passengers grab armrests. They take deep breaths. The nose of the plane tilts up. Tom licks his lips. The wheels are a hundred feet from the ground. Tom whispers into her ear.

'What would make this perfect?' he whispers.

The Perfectionist stops. She turns her head, slightly, in his direction. Fifty feet. Tom whispers again, even softer, even quieter.

'Perf, what would make this moment perfect?'

He leans his forehead against hers. Their foreheads touch. Without making a sound, Tom mouths the words again, 'What would make this perfect?'

And she sees him.

THE COMPENDIUM OF SUPERHEROES, GREATER TORONTO AREA

INTRODUCTION

It's been ten years since Tom and the Perfectionist landed safely in Vancouver. I can't believe that much time has passed. So much has happened and yet nothing has changed. Tom and the Perfectionist bought a house. They had two kids, a boy and a girl.

They got jobs and tired, argued and made up, became baffled and stronger and maybe just a little bit wiser. But the truth is that the life they're leading, while unquestionably weird, is for the most part incredibly ordinary.

For this special tenth anniversary edition we're returning to the city of Toronto, to present 32 more of the 249 super-heroes who frequent our city. Each one of these superheroes is special yet common, gifted yet clumsy, triumphant yet sad, simultaneously extraordinary and common.

Just like you and just like me.

FORMER ROOMMATES
OF THE PERFECTIONIST

THE BEDMAKER

Every morning the Bedmaker wakes up beside the man she loves and has loved since she was sixteen. She gently wakes him up. She watches him go downstairs to make coffee. She swings out her legs and puts her toes to the cold floor, and as she stands her bed is instantly made behind her. The sheets become clean. The pillows are fluffed and set against the headboard. The comforter lies flat and creaseless, and all confusion, regret, resentment and doubt fall from her heart.

MS FRAZZLED

When Ms Frazzled shared the top floor of a once-stately home, now turned into four apartments, on Palmerston Blvd., she went by the name Ms Cool. Now she has three children, aged eight, six and two.

SMALLDIFFERENCE

Have you ever gotten a speeding ticket and then wondered what would've happened if you hadn't stopped to tie your shoes? How would things have been different if you'd caught that green light? Or if you hadn't decided to go back and answer your phone when you heard it ringing? Smalldifference can tell you: it would make no difference at all. This is her superpower: the ability to tell you that it wouldn't have changed a thing.

THE ATTENTION SEEKER

There are many things the Attention Seeker isn't good at. In truth, there is little that comes naturally to her. She burns dinners, gets fired for failing to detect shoplifters and cannot fly. That is unless her husband is pouring her a glass of wine and talking about his day in the kitchen, or her boss is on the floor and looking for someone to promote, or her son wants to act out a scene from the comic book he's reading. Under these conditions, her roast will drip off the bone, she knows who to watch and catches them in the act, she opens the third-storey window and confidently dives out with her son on her back. The Attention Seeker can do just about anything, and do it better than just about anyone, as long as it gives her the attention she's seeking.

HYPNO'S SHORT-TERM
RELATIONSHIPS

THE ALARMIST

The Alarmist was born with every emergency number already memorized. An escape route pops into her head the moment she enters each and every building. Her panic room is impenetrable, well stocked and tested quarterly for every imaginable crisis, from blackout to meteor, intruder to atomic blast. She's prepared for the worst: any worst, anytime. She's constantly disappointed that it never happens.

THE INSECURITY MONSTER

Doris Thermen is a wispy twig of a girl, just under five feet tall and ninety-eight pounds, who occasionally transforms into a seven-foot creature with long pointed teeth and razor-sharp fingernails who's covered in shocking orange hair. Known as the Insecurity Monster, her metamorphosis occurs whenever she isn't the centre of attention. The change is, however, so stunning that no one can look away, provoking the Insecurity Monster to change back into the wispy twig of Doris Thermen.

THE BOYBENDER

Is it an incredibly successful system of subtle suggestions and rewards? Maybe the accumulation by prolonged proximity of an unconscious desire? Perhaps the weight of impossible standards and unrealistic expectations? Nobody knows. All that's certain is how every man the Boybender falls in love with begins to look the same. First they begin dressing in fine suits, without a tie. Then their faces begin to morph. Their noses grow longer or shorter, their chins sharper or less so, their eyes get closer together or farther apart. Then they either shrink or grow in height and before long they all look exactly like her father.

ZENITH

Although sexually active in the later years of high school, Zenith didn't discover her superpower until she was in university. After the end of a three-year relationship, Zenith had a bout of sleeping around and word spread fast. No matter how great the sex you've had is, sex with Zenith will be better. This is her superpower. Now no one will go to bed with her. Who wants to know, for sure and without a doubt, that it's all downhill from there?

SUPERHEROES THE CLOCK
HAS DUMPED
(but not until three years in)

THE JUMPER

The Jumper has jumped aboard, ahead and to conclusions. He's jumped into love and out of the frying pan. He's jumped trains, girls and bail. No one can jump into, or out of, things like he can.

It's an ability equalled only by his failure to stick around long enough to accomplish anything.

MAINCHARACTER

Refused to be included in this compendium.

MIRRORRORRIM

The first time it happened he was twenty-six and on a first date with Jessica Hawkins. This first date reminded him of his very first date, ten years earlier, with Angie McCurdy. Three days later he was getting a haircut, which reminded him of the haircut he'd received a month earlier. That evening he was barbecuing a steak in his backyard when he remembered a barbecue in Alana Burton's backyard.

Then the taste of his beer reminded him of a bluegrass festival he'd gone to in university. Then going to bed made him remember going to bed the night before. And then it happened: remembering going to bed the night before caused him to remember remembering Christmas dinner, 1997.

Now all he does is sit in a chair, remembering the moments when he remembered other moments.

NEVERWRONG

Have you ever had an argument in which you were so sure of yourself, in which, without a doubt, you knew something to be true? That searing meat seals in flavour? Or that the Great Wall of China is the only man-made object visible from the moon? Or that bats are blind? But then you checked the Internet and discovered that searing may actually make meat lose moisture. That the Apollo astronauts reported seeing no man-made objects other then the lights of major cities. That, while bats do use echolocation as a primary sense, all species have eyes and are perfectly capable of sight.

Most likely, you were arguing with Neverwrong, a man with the ability to change the world in order to win an argument.

STRESS BUNNY'S LEAGUE OF LOSERS

THE WORKHOUSE

The Workhorse is the first to arrive at the office and the last to leave. He doesn't look up when you walk past him at the end of the day. Weekends, holidays and birthdays are all spent at work.

His loyalty to the corporation is unquestioned and unsurpassed. But he has never received either a raise or a promotion because his bosses figure that anyone working that hard is surely incompetent, lucky just to have a job.

THE PHONY

The telephone is his weapon. Over it he'll make plans for lunch dates and movies. He'll set the date as 'maybe Thursday,' or 'I'll call on Tuesday,' or 'sometime next week.' But then Thursday comes and you haven't heard from him. Tuesday arrives but his phone call hasn't. It's next week and there's been no lunch date or movie – just the dull realization that the Phony has struck again.

THE FORCED

He can explain something that's happened to you in a way that you've never thought of it before, a way that offers wisdom and insight, a fresh perspective you would never have thought of on your own – but he can only do it using quotes, characters and situations from Star Wars.

THE TINY GIANT

The Tiny Giant stands eight and a half feet tall. He can take a half-flight of stairs in a single step, has never failed to catch a bus he's running after, and can paint ceilings without a ladder. However, he is the shortest in his family, having three brothers who all stand over nine feet tall. He went to a special school for giants, where the average height was nine feet, four inches. His house was specially constructed for a giant, but one who is taller than he is. So while he doesn't have to crouch in the living room or duck under doorways, he has to stand on a chair to reach the top shelf.

Because of these things, the Tiny Giant considers himself a small man, even while stooping to stand on the streetcar, helping cats stuck in trees or vying for the object of his affection.

POWER COUPLES

THE PREVARICATOR & YOU'RERIGHT!

The Prevaricator was born with the power to look at every single issue from every single perspective, to consider every single opinion. His life was a series of failures, unfinished projects and extended, demoralizing debates, mainly with himself. His power simply depressed everybody. He couldn't decide what to do about it, what to do with himself, until he met You'reRight.

You'reRight was born with the power to say yes to absolutely everything. She said yes to a date, yes to his desires and then yes when he asked her to marry him. They had a couple of rough patches but then, when she said yes to making all the decisions, things improved, greatly, and the Prevaricator finally became happy.

MAYBESOON & WE'LLSEE

MaybeSoon fell in love with We'llSee. All of their friends were already married so they got married too. But when all of their friends started having children, MaybeSoon and We'llSee decided not to. Children just weren't for them. MaybeSoon had just been made partner and We'llSee's dress shop was finally turning a profit. They were short of time, not money, so they bought a second home out in the country, with twenty acres and stables, so they could have horses.

The first night they stayed in their new country home they made love. They were careful. They weren't careful enough. The next morning We'llSee knew. She just knew. It seemed ludicrous, this knowing, so she waited for twelve days. Then she waited seven more days. Then she bought a kit. She locked the bathroom door. She peed on it. A blue cross slowly formed. She called MaybeSoon at the office and to her surprise he was as excited as she was. Eleven months later she gave birth to twin horses.

THE GREAT EVERYWHERE & STAYATHOME

The Great Everywhere was a very tired man. Being at every art opening, at every cool concert and book launch, and shooting a cameo for every independent movie being filmed in Toronto was exhausting him. Yet he could not stop. Meanwhile, Stayathome had begun to find herself and her life more than a little dull. While she enjoyed her evenings reading on the couch, soft music playing in the background, Cab Sauv in her glass, she had begun to feel like she needed something more. They met at the laundromat, hit it off and, to the surprise of both, slept together that night. It was while they were doing so that their powers merged, perfectly balancing each other, giving each the ultimate power: knowing exactly when to stay home and when to go out.

They are, by far, the most successful couple in Toronto.

NOILLUSIONS & FACETHETRUTH

Debbie Wilson packed herself into her husband's suitcase to make sure he was going where he claimed to be going. It was a tight fit. To make enough room for herself she removed most of his clothes, which she hid underneath the bed. Then she curled up into a ball. She used the nail on her right index finger to close the zipper from the inside. She remained silent as he carried her to the cab and put the suitcase in the trunk.

At first there was a tiny point of light in the space where she couldn't get the zipper all the way closed. Then the trunk was slammed shut and she lost this too. The darkness was complete. It was hard to keep track of time. She was jostled around. She felt the weight of many other bags on top of her. Eventually she fell asleep. When she woke up she was moving in a large oval and then she was lifted upwards and she knew that her husband had collected her.

A car ride followed. She was carried inside a room and set on the floor. She heard the door close.

'I'm so sorry I'm late!' her husband said.

'You're not that late,' a female voice said. Their talking continued. It was intimate. It was clear what was going on. Debbie wanted to unzip right there and confront her husband, confront them both, but the knowledge that her husband was fooling around made her weak. She stayed in the dark and listened and she was forced to hear everything there was to hear. She waited until they'd both showered and left the room and only then did she unzip. When she emerged, she was no longer Debbie Wilson. She had become NoIllusions.

The first thing NoIllusions noticed was the other suitcase. She assumed it belonged to the other woman. She stared at it in hatred and then it began to unzip. NoIllusions saw a hand. The hand was male. Next came his arm and then his shoulder and then the head and face. The man stood up. He looked at her and then he looked at her husband's unzipped suitcase.

'Was that your wife?' NoIllusions asked him.

'For now,' the man said. Earlier this morning, when he'd zipped himself in to his wife's suitcase, his name had been Brian Davidson. As he looked at NoIllusions he knew that his name was FaceTheTruth.

'Was that your husband?' he asked.

'Not for long.'

They looked at each other and they recognized something. Maybe it was just the circumstances of how they met, but they didn't think so. This felt deeper than that. They talked for a while about where they grew up, what their parents were like. They held hands. Then they sat on the edge of the bed and kissed. They didn't do anything more than that. It didn't seem necessary. It seemed like something they should save for later. In soap, on the mirror in the bathroom, they wrote,

We know this is weird but we'd honestly like to thank you for bringing us together.

Then they left the room, hand in hand.

THE AMPHIBIAN'S CLOSEST FRIENDS,
AFTER TOM

MR LATE

Mr Late will always be late. You can count on it. You can lie to him, tell him to be there at 7:00 when you really need him to be there at 7:30, but he won't arrive until 8:00. You cannot outsmart him. You will simply have to wait. You'll stand there, waiting, and you'll get so bored that you'll call your mom and something about having time to kill will put you in a chatty mood and you'll connect with her in a way you haven't since you left home for university. Or you'll sit down on a bench and suddenly there, right at eye level, will be a poster for a garage sale. It's happening three doors down from your house next Saturday, so you go and you find that record, the one you used to have when you were a teenager, the one you've been looking for for years. You buy it for a dollar and when you listen to it you rediscover a side of yourself that you'd forgotten, a kinder, gentler, more optimistic version of yourself. This is Mr Late's superpower: he will always be late but something of great importance will happen to you while you're waiting for him. It is, however, still extremely annoying.

LUCKY

Every time Lucky goes to park his car, a spot opens up right in front of the building he's about to go inside. He never pays for parking and he never gets a ticket. He arrives at every restaurant just as they've had a cancellation and the best table in the house is suddenly free. His planes are never delayed, he always performs best when the boss is around and he married a woman whose love and forgiveness are inexhaustible.

However, he firmly believes that everyone, at birth, is given a finite amount of luck. So each time something lucky happens to him, which is almost every minute of every day, he curses it, convinced he's another step closer to his luck running out.

THE INEVITABLE WOMAN

It started when she heard herself using odd phrases, like calling dinner 'supper' and describing her gay friends as 'going up the down staircase.' Then her wardrobe began to change: her hemlines got longer and her jeans got higher waisted. She could no longer stand to drink cheap wine and then Friday night became an opportunity to just stay home, watch tv and relax. Shortly after she bought a reliable car that got good mileage, she looked in the mirror and discovered that she had become her mother.

THE BIG GOODBYE

Maybe you're about to get a new job, or a divorce, or else the friendship has run its course and you've started moving in different social circles: whatever it is, the Big Goodbye already knows about it. She'll shake your hand and look you in the eye and there will just be something about the way she does it. Her grip will be a little tighter than usual, or her eyes will be a little moist, or her voice will squeak a bit. Nothing major –in fact, nothing you would even notice until months later, when you look back, and you realize that that was the last time you ever saw the Big Goodbye.

SUPERHEROES TOM WISHES HE WERE

MR FIX-IT

Although completely useless as a handyman, Mr Fix-It can repair anybody, anytime. He can pinpoint the exact cause of your unhappiness and suggest the perfect solution. He will look in your eyes, see that the problem is loneliness, and provide the phone number of a person you should immediately start dating. He has a contact at a company currently in need of someone with exactly your skill set. He knows a karate class you should enroll your son in to help build his self-confidence.

But no one goes on the blind dates he sets up. No one applies for the jobs he recommends. The sons end up playing soccer. All of which has forced Mr Fix-It to conclude that no one really wants their problems to be solved. Without them, he believes, no one would have any idea who they are.

SLEEPONIT

No matter how stressful the situation, or how big the decision, or how filled with anxiety she is, come 10:10 p.m. Sleeponit will climb into bed and immediately fall asleep. She will sleep soundly, with no interruptions. At 7:15 a.m. she'll wake up, stretch and know exactly what to do.

FLUKE

If he's not in a hurry, the first taxi that passes will stop. If he doesn't really want the job, he'll ace the interview and be offered a position. The day he's happy being single is the day he'll fall in love at first sight. Fluke can get anything, easily, without effort, as long as he really doesn't really want it.

RUNNINGONEMPTY

Runningonempty is perpetually doing just that. She's got $78.00 in her bank account. Her only pair of boots has a hole in the left sole. Her hair, while it doesn't grow, is constantly in need of a cut. No matter how early she leaves, something happens – a flat tyre, construction – that makes her fifteen minutes late. And yet she never fails to pay her rent and she never runs out of gas and she always, somehow, arrives. Although times are continuously hard, Runningonempty is one of the very few superheroes who is, and who will always remain, unstoppable.

ACKNOWLEDGEMENTS

The author wishes to thank:

Shirley Kaufman, Rolly Kaufman and Liz Kaufman for decades of support and encouragement. We are a family so nuclear we glow. Zachariah Pickard, Suzanne Matczuk and especially Alana Wilcox whose brilliant ideas and insights into the editing of this book were so accurate and knowing, the reader thinks it's all me. Allen Sherwood, Andy Pedersen, Tom Barkhouse, Stephanie Domet, Matt Tunnacliffe, Chris Boyce and everybody at dnto, Rob McLaughlin and everybody at cbc Radio 3, Karrie North, Karen and Barry Miazga, Ian McInnis, Jason McBride, Sheila Heti, Nora Young and Marc Forrest for support over the long, long, long haul. And, of course, Marlo Miazga (a superhero name if ever there was one).

ABOUT THE AUTHOR

Andrew Kaufman was born in the town of Wingham, Ontario. This is the same town that Alice Munro was born in, making him the secondbest writer from a town of 3,000. Descending from a long line of librarians and accountants, his first published work was *All My Friends Are Superheroes*, which has been translated into Italian, French, Norwegian, German, Korean, Spanish, Dutch, Portuguese, Catalan, Swedish and Turkish. He has since published *The Waterproof Bible*, *The Tiny Wife*, *Selected Business Correspondence* and *Born Weird*. He is also an accomplished screenwriter for film and television, and has completed a Director's Residence at the Canadian Film Centre. He lives in downtown Toronto with his wife, the film editor Marlo Miazga, and their two children, Phoenix and Frida.

TV GIRL

THE AMPHIBIAN

THE EAR

RUNNINGONEMPTY

THE SPOONER

someday

THE GAMBLER

THE JUMPER

THE BATTERY

Heart Repair

AMBROSE
HEART-REPAIR

THE IMPOSSIBLE MAN

JENNY
REMINGTON

THE INSECURITY
MONSTER

HYPNO